15 things NOT to do with a Granny

Margaret McAllister

Illustrated by Holly Sterling

Frances Lincoln
Children's Books

A **granny** is a wonderful person to have in your life. If you're really lucky, you might have two grannies.

Follow these simple rules to make sure every granny is a happy granny.

Don't...

hide an **elephant** in your granny's bed.

Don't...

give her **squashed jelly beans** on toast for breakfast,

or put leftover **spaghetti** in her handbag.

Don't...

wear her **pants** on your head,

or use her **make-up** on your teddy bear.

Don't...

race her on a **skateboard**.

(She might win.)

Don't...

give her a **crocodile** for her birthday,

or interrupt her doing **karate**.

Don't...

bang a **drum** to wake her up.

In fact, don't make any **loud noises**
when she's resting.

Don't... ask her to read too
many **books** at once,

or forget to **share** her.

Don't...

send her up to the **moon** in a rocket.

Never...

swap her for a giraffe,

or **someone else's granny.**

DO...

go for walks,

listen to her,

play,

sing,

hug your granny,

help your granny,

and most of all...

...love her. Lots.
She loves you!